Kathryn Lasky • ***Illustrated by* Mitch Vane**

Poodle and Hound

Charlesbridge

To my granddaughter, Lulu Knight,
and her good friend, Hanzo

—K. L.

For Bonny and Stella

—M. V.

2011 First paperback edition

Published by Charlesbridge
85 Main Street
Watertown, MA 02472
(617) 926-0329
www.charlesbridge.com

Library of Congress Cataloging-in-Publication Data
Lasky, Kathryn.
Poodle and Hound / Kathryn Lasky ; illustrated by Mitch Vane.
p. cm.
Summary: In three adventures, Hound and Poodle discover how much they enjoy each other's company, in spite of, or maybe because of, their differences.
ISBN 978-1-58089-322-0 (reinforced for library use)
ISBN 978-1-58089-323-7 (softcover)
[1. Friendship—Fiction. 2. Dogs—Fiction.] I. Vane, Mitch, ill. II. Title.
PZ7.L3274Pom 2009
[E]—dc22 2008025343

Printed in China
(hc) 10 9 8 7 6 5 4 3 2 1
(sc) 10 9 8 7 6 5 4 3 2 1

Illustrations done in watercolor and dip pen and India ink on Bockingford watercolor paper
Display type and text type set in Cafe Mimi, Bokka, and Baskerville MT
Color separations by Chroma Graphics, Singapore
Printed and bound September 2010 in Nansha, Guangdong, China, by Everbest Printing Company, Ltd. through Four Colour Imports Ltd., Louisville, Kentucky
Production supervision by Brian G. Walker
Designed by Diane M. Earley

Contents

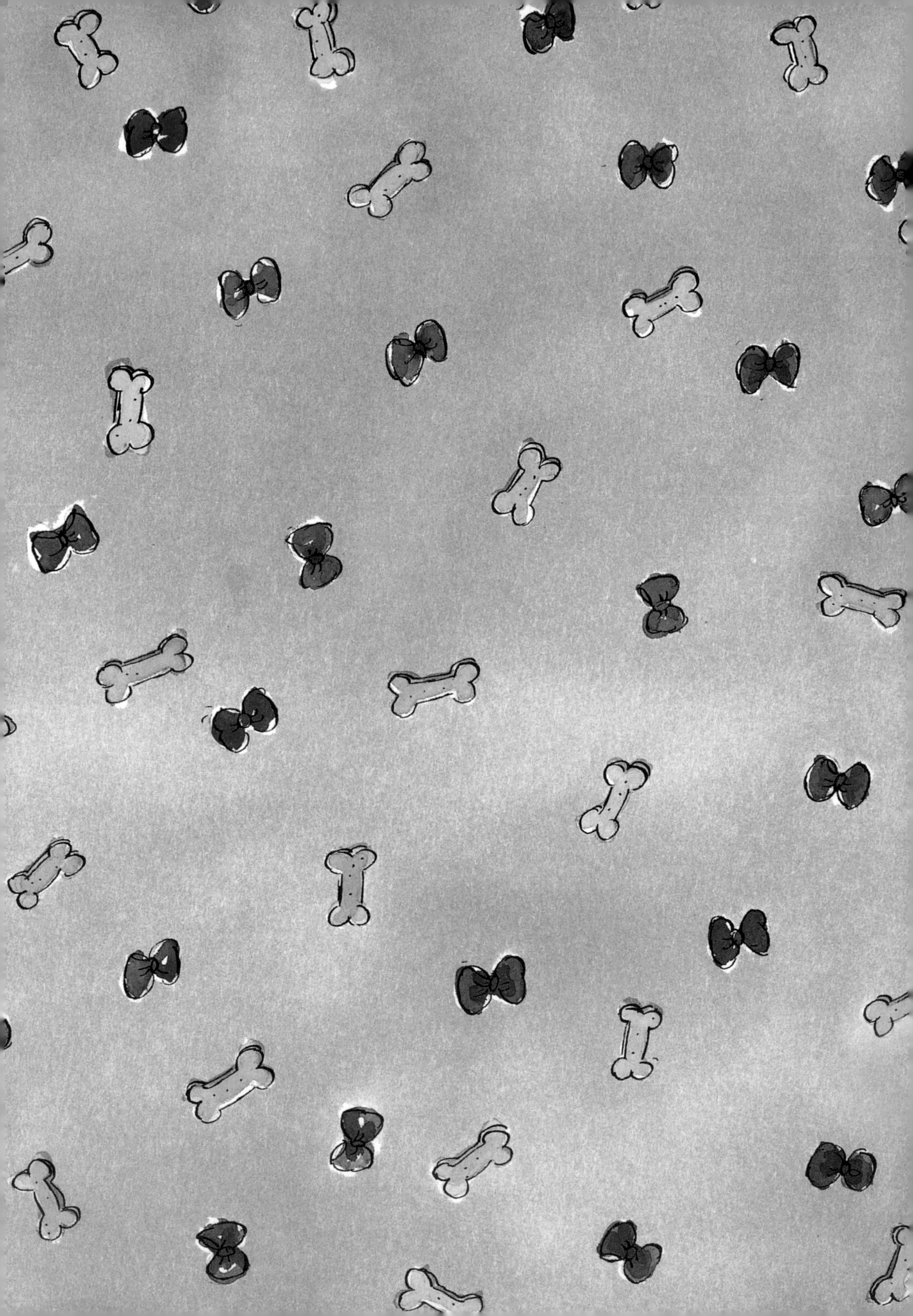

Beauty

One day Poodle decided to have her fur done.

"I am going to the beauty salon, Hound," she announced. "I will be back later." Hound did not look up from his newspaper.

At the beauty salon Poodle had her fur trimmed into pom-poms. A stunning fur ball stood on the very tip-top of her head.

She looked at herself in the mirror and said, "Lovely!"

Poodle thought her feet and ears looked particularly fetching.

"Elegant," she said with a sigh.

Then she thought, "All this beauty will be wasted on Hound." So Poodle trotted downtown to the Ritz for tea.

Poodle insisted on having a table by the window. She wanted to be admired from both the outside and inside of the restaurant. Poodle ordered tea and a plate of cookies.

"Ooh, yummy!" she exclaimed after she bit into the first cookie. The two corgis at the next table looked at her in alarm.

"Oh, dear," Poodle thought. "They must think I am crazy, talking to myself." So she sat up straight and proper and quietly ate her cookies and sipped her tea.

“I wonder if anyone is looking at me?” Poodle asked herself. “Are they admiring my pom-poms?” She looked around slyly. Everyone was busy talking. Poodle kept eating. She began to think about Hound.

“Hound would love these chocolate cookies,” she said aloud. The two corgis looked at her again.

“Oh, I am sorry. I—” Poodle began to apologize, but then she stopped. Why was she apologizing to them? Why couldn’t she sit here with her bows and pom-poms and talk out loud if she wanted? She could sing out loud if she wanted! By gum!

So Poodle did just that. She hummed a soft little tune about Hound.

RITZ

I'm so sorry Hound's not here.
He would add a bit of cheer.

He's not exactly pretty,
But he's sure not dumb.
Life without him
is especially glum!

Then she added with a little moan,

I feel so alone.
I must trot along home.

So she did.

"Poodle!" Hound exclaimed as she came through the door. "You look lovely."

He put down his newspaper.

"Really, Hound?"

“Those bows . . . those pom-poms . . . your adorable ears . . . and that bit of fluff on your paws!”

“Oh, Hound, I thought you would not notice!” Poodle was shocked.

“Nothing is ever wasted on a friend, Poodle,” Hound said wisely.

“Oh, Hound. I saved a cookie just for you. Let us have tea.”

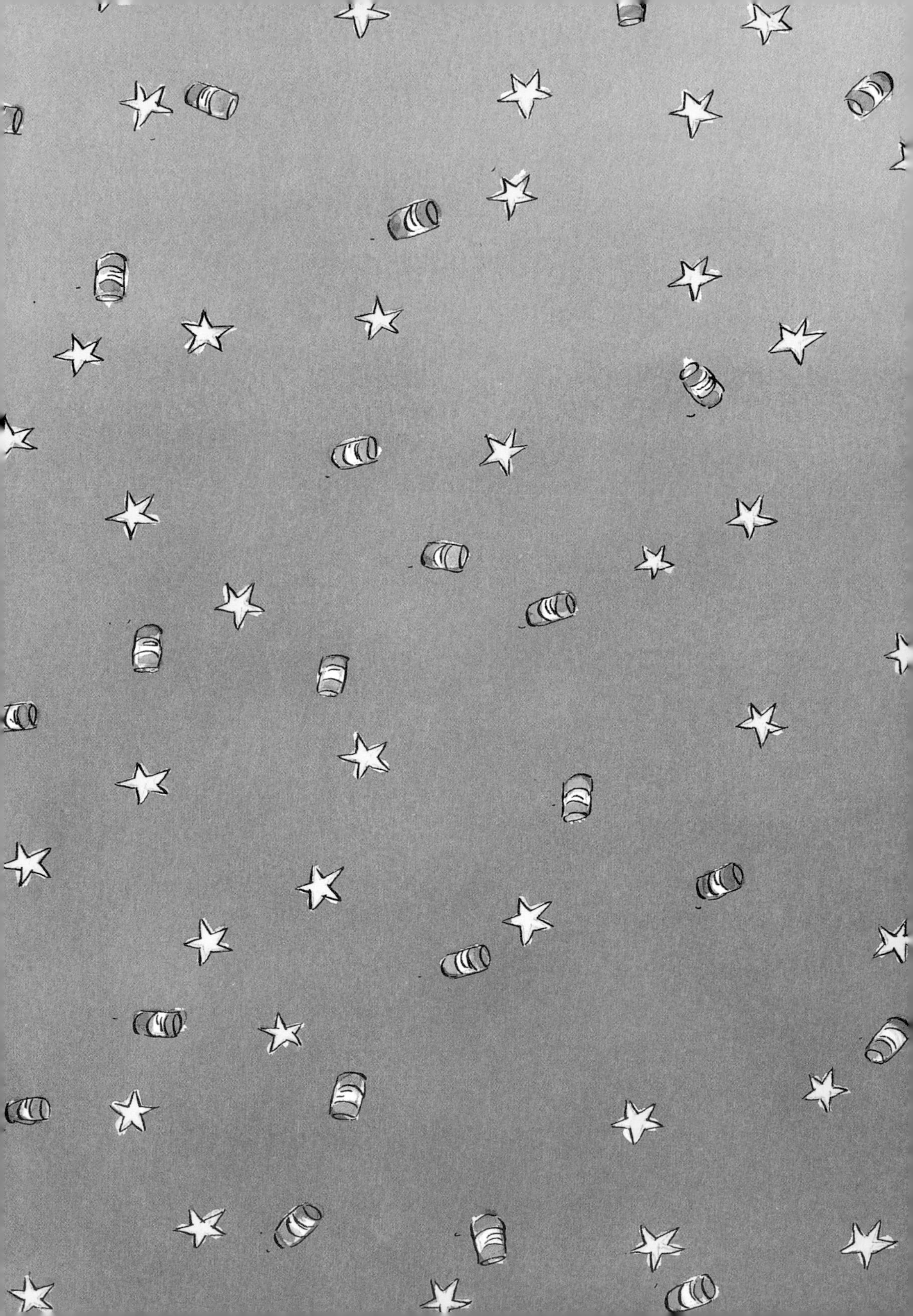

Starry Night

One starry night Hound was looking through his telescope. He looked at the sky. He wrote down numbers on pieces of paper.

Poodle came up to join him. "I can't sleep, Hound. What are you doing?"

"I am counting stars and comparing the brightness of planets. I am hoping to see the rings of Saturn and the moons of Jupiter." He wrote down more numbers.

Hound wished that Poodle would not distract him.

"That is not fair," Poodle whimpered.

"What is not fair?" Hound asked.

"You have something to do and I do not."

"Well, you can look at the stars, too," Hound said.

"The stars are far away. There is only one telescope," Poodle replied.

"We could share it," Hound said. He crossed out a number. It was hard to think.

"Okay, my turn," Poodle said.

"No, not yet. This is very important work," Hound replied. He had just caught sight of a new star. He looked at a chart.

"Ooh, that is a pretty star!" Poodle exclaimed.

"Sssh—I need to concentrate." Hound mumbled some numbers to himself. Then he scribbled on a piece of paper and frowned.

"Hound, I am bored. B-O-R-E-D. May I have a turn?"

Poodle could be so annoying. "How do you expect me to calculate the brightness of this star properly?"

Poodle sniffed. She reached for the telescope.

"Hold on," Hound said. "I think I can see the Sea of Tranquility on the Moon." Oh, how he wished Poodle would go to bed. He heard her sigh loudly, and it was not a yawn.

"You know, Hound, it was not always so peaceful up there in the Moon's Sea of Tranquility."

"Really?" Hound asked.

"It is true," Poodle replied. "Put away that star chart thing and listen.

"Once upon a time," she began, "there were monsters on the Moon. They lived happily in the Sea of Tranquility. There was a mommy monster, a daddy monster, and twin baby monsters. They breathed moonlight and ate stardust.

"But one night some snakes from another galaxy slithered through space and invaded the Moon!

"There was a big fight between the snakes and the monsters. It looked as if the snakes were winning, because they had tied the monsters in knots. But then . . ."

The story grew more and more exciting. Not once did Hound look through the telescope. He didn't write on his papers or pick up his star charts. Finally Poodle came to the end of the story.

"And that is also how Saturn got its rings. They are really frozen snakes flung from the Moon by the monsters. At last the Moon's sea is tranquil."

“Wow,” Hound gasped. “That is fantastic! You are some storyteller, Poodle. Did you make that up all by yourself?”

“Yep,” Poodle answered.

“Do you want to look through the telescope now?” Hound asked.

“No. Telling stories about the stars is more fun.”

“I think you should be a writer, Poodle. You have a gift.”

“Do you really think so, Hound?”

"Oh, yes," Hound said. He sat down next to Poodle.

Poodle's words began to wind into the night. The two friends stayed up late, whispering of stars and moons and planets with strange rings.

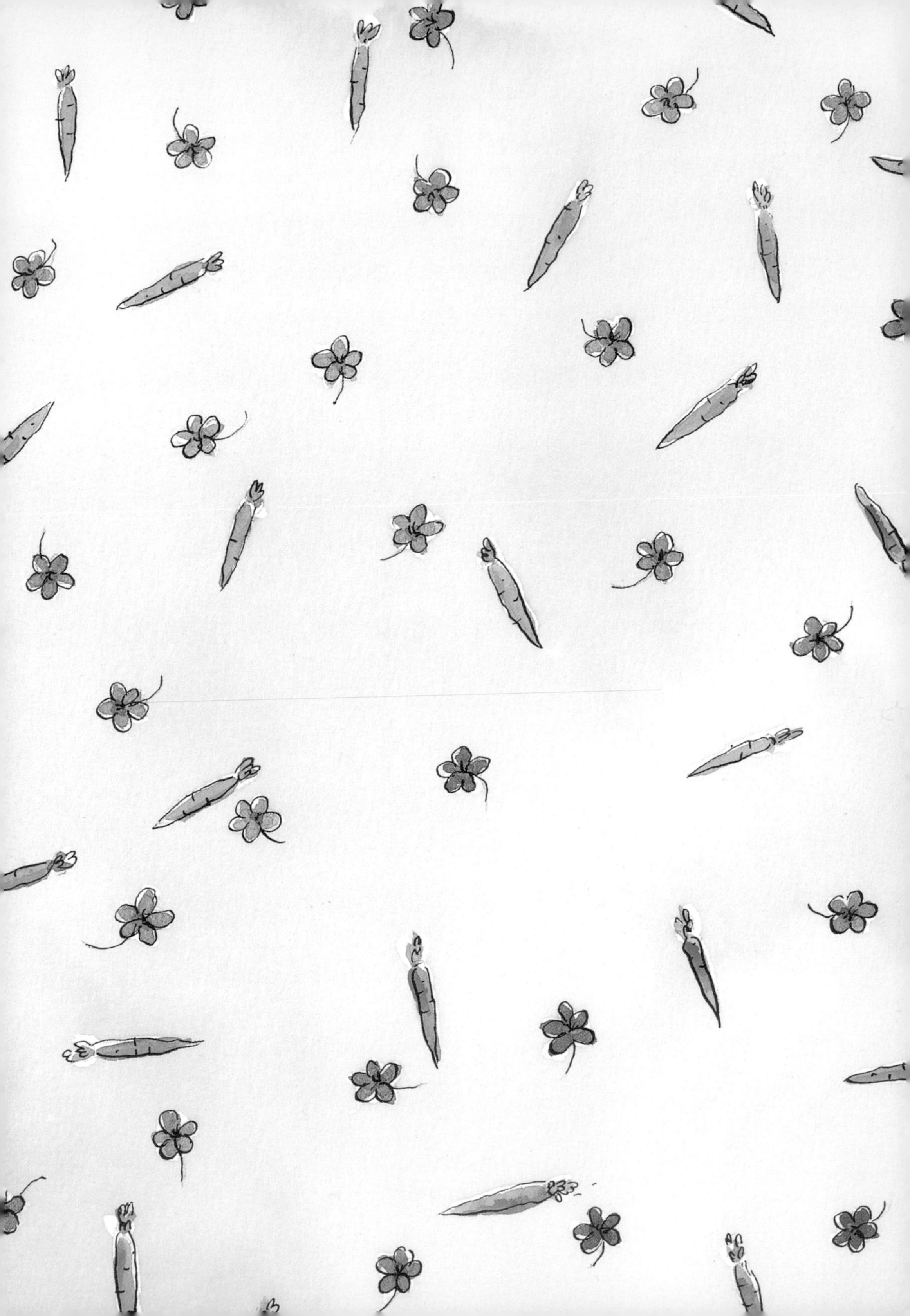

The Garden

"I am going to plant a garden," Hound said. He took out a big piece of paper and crayons.

"Hound," Poodle said, "that is not *planting* a garden. That is *drawing* a garden."

"The first step in planting a garden is planning. I shall make a drawing to show where each vegetable will grow," Hound said.

"Just vegetables? We must have absolutely fabulous flowers."

“Poodle,” Hound said sternly, “flowers are not in the plan. Besides, they are not nutritious.”

He began to draw tiny pictures. He drew beets, carrots, radishes, and tomatoes. Then he drew cucumbers, beans, melons, and five kinds of lettuce.

“Boring,” Poodle muttered under her breath. She decided to go to the library. She wanted to read something exciting.

At the library Poodle saw a new book called *Bad Bugs and Thugs: Put Pests to Rest.*

"What is this about?" she asked the librarian.

"It is about the bad bugs that wreck gardens, and the good bugs that keep them away."

Poodle sat right down and started reading. It was shocking how bad bugs could be!

Thank goodness there were also good bugs. It turned out that gardeners could attract these hero bugs by planting certain kinds of flowers.

"This is fantastic," Poodle said. "I can help Hound and get my flowers, too!"

Poodle made a chart:

Bad Bugs that eat vegetables	Good Bugs that scare Bad Bugs	Flowers that Good Bugs like
aphids	ladybugs	yarrow
leafhoppers	lacewings	daisies
mealbugs	hoverflies	marigolds
spidermites	pirate bugs	sunflowers

After making many lists and drawings, Hound was ready to plant the garden.

"What about garden security, Hound?" Poodle asked.

"Security?" Hound asked.

"There are bad critters out there, Hound," Poodle said in a serious voice. "I read all about them. They will eat your vegetables. They will nibble the lettuce and make holes in the potatoes."

“What are we going to do, Poodle?”

Hound asked.

"Don't worry. I am planning a surprise attack on the bad critters. Top secret," Poodle said.

Poodle began planting seeds. She put in rows of daisies, yarrow, and marigolds. These flowers would attract good bugs that would eat the bad bugs.

"Take that, you bug thugs!" Poodle said as she watered the seeds.

Weeks later Hound noticed a small green sprout in the garden.

"Is that a weed?" he asked.

"Don't touch it!" Poodle shrieked. "It is part of the surprise attack. Have patience. P-A-T-I-E-N-C-E. It will grow bigger."

The sprout did grow bigger and bigger, along with everything else. The tomatoes got redder. The beet leaves got bushier. The flowers bloomed brightly.

One day a carrot was ready to eat.

Next came a small squash.

"I have never been able to grow so many vegetables, Poodle," Hound said. "It must have been your surprise attack. What did you do?"

Poodle showed him her charts. She explained the plan that she had made.

"That is really clever, Poodle!" Hound exclaimed. "Let us celebrate with a garden feast."

The two friends picked vegetables.

They scrubbed the dirt from the squash and peeled the cucumbers.

They made a salad with five kinds of lettuce.

Finally it was time to sit down.

"This is lovely," Poodle said. "It was worth the wait."

"Can you wait just one more minute, Poodle?" Hound asked.

"Oh, Hound!" Poodle protested.

"Patience! One minute, please," Hound begged.

"Oh, all right," Poodle said.

Hound came back with a bouquet of flowers.

"Poodle, thank you for showing me that flowers are a vegetable's best friend," he said.

Poodle looked at the flowers that Hound had brought to the table. She looked at the feast they were about to eat.

"Garden friends," she whispered. She put a marigold behind her ear. "Now, what will we plant next year, Hound?"

"I thought you would never ask, Poodle," Hound said. He pulled out the new plans from his back pocket.